Homes in the Sea

PROPERTY OF SPOTSYLVANIA
COUNTY SCHOOL BOARD
CHAPTER II

PROJECT NO. _088-C2-87_

SCHOOL YEAR DATE _26 - 86/87_

Homes in the Sea
From the Shore to the Deep

by Jean H. Sibbald

Dillon Press, Inc.   Minneapolis, Minnesota 55415

To Julie

Library of Congress Cataloging in Publication Data

Sibbald, Jean H.
  Homes in the sea : from the shore to the deep.

  Bibliography: p.
  Includes index.
  Summary: An introduction to the various animals that inhabit
the sea.
  1. Marine fauna—Habitat—Juvenile literature.
2. Marine biology—Juvenile literature. [1. Marine animals.
2. Marine biology] I. Title.
QL122.2.S53   1985   574.92   85-6865
ISBN 0-87518-304-2

Dillon Press, Inc., 242 Portland Avenue South
Minneapolis, Minnesota 55415

Printed in the United States of America
1 2 3 4 5 6 7 8 9 10 93 92 91 90 89 88 87 86

Contents

 Sea Facts

Size:

140,000,000 square miles (361,000,000 square kilometers)—71 percent of the earth's surface

Greatest Depth:

6.8 miles (10.9 kilometers)

Surface Temperature:

Highest—95°F (35°C)
Lowest—29.5°F (-1.4°C), the freezing point of seawater

Different Species of Sea Animals:

Fishes—30,000
Shellfish—47,000
Sponges—3,000
Crabs and their kin—25,000
Corals and their kin—5,000
Starfish and their kin—6,000

Different Species of Seaweeds:

10,000

Length of Coastline:

    In the continental USA—54,000 miles (86,400 kilometers)

    In the world—1,000,000 miles (1,600,000 kilometers)

Largest Creature in the Sea:

    Blue whale (110 feet or 33.5 meters long; 150 tons or 135 metric tons in weight)

Largest Plant in the Sea:

    Giant kelp (100 feet or 30.5 meters long)

 Introduction

Thousands of different kinds of creatures live in the sea. There are fish, **shellfish**,* **marine worms**, **corals**, and **sponges**. There are strange looking creatures with **tentacles**, jointed legs, or pointed tails. They do not look like the animals on land at all, yet they are animals—sea animals. Some are so small that they can be seen only through a **microscope**. Others, such as some whales, are larger than the biggest animals on land.

Like land animals, sea creatures must have their own special places to live. Some hide in caves or holes or among waving strands of seaweed. Others dig or bore into sand, wood, or even rock. Many live on the sea bed, on or in the sand or mud. Some sea creatures settle in one spot and never stray. Others roam the open sea, like cattle on the range, moving wherever conditions are suitable for their lives.

The sea offers an enormous area for animal life. It covers almost three-quarters of the surface of the

*Words in **bold type** are explained in the glossary at the end of this book.

Coral polyps. (Ken Howard/ EarthViews)

earth. At its deepest point, it reaches 6.8 miles (10.9 kilometers) down, deeper than the height of the highest mountain on land. Wherever the sea reaches, animals of some kind can be found.

Many conditions affect the sea **environment** and the suitability of any particular place for life. Temperature, wave action, light, and **salinity**, or amount of salt in the water, are all important. So, too, are the depth of the sea and the amount of **oxygen** in the water. Above all, food must be available.

Each sea creature is adapted to living in certain conditions. Some are comfortable in many different kinds of locations. Some are able to withstand great changes in their environment. Others have such particular needs that even a minor change in their surroundings will force them to move or die. Whatever their needs, sea creatures choose their homes accordingly.

Caves, Crevices and Cans

Sea creatures that like small, dark places make their homes in caves and **crevices**. Such homes are in and under rocks and shells, or among the broken timbers of a sunken ship. Even thrown-away cans and jars become tiny caves for sea creatures.

Octopus

The octopus is a cave dweller. This strange and forbidding creature appears to be all head and arms. What looks like the top of a bald head, however, is really the bag-shaped body. Between the body and the arms is a small head with two bulging yellowish eyes. Eight long arms, or tentacles, hang in a circle from the octopus's head, hiding the mouth underneath.

The long arms dwarf the octopus's body, giving it a fearsome look. Most of the creatures are timid and harmless, however. The common octopus may grow to four or five feet when measured from tip to tip of its outstretched arms. Some kinds never grow larger

An octopus uses its long tentacles to capture a crab. (Allan Roberts)

than your hand. The largest type of octopus reaches more than thirty feet (nine meters) from arm tip to arm tip. Even this huge creature has a body only a foot long. But what amazingly long tentacles it has!

An octopus can change from one color to another at will. It may be brown at one time and light gray or reddish at another. It can change from spotted to striped or to half one color and half another.

If threatened, the octopus squirts out a cloud of inklike fluid that hides it as it darts quickly away. By a kind of jet propulsion, or power, the octopus swishes rapidly this way and that, body forward and arms trailing behind.

During the day, the octopus hides in its dark and cozy lair. At night it ventures forth, searching for a dinner of crabs and small shellfish. It can pull itself along on its long arms, or stretch its arms downward and walk on the slightly curled tips as if they were small feet. Gathering a supply of shellfish, the octopus takes them home for a leisurely meal.

Moray Eel

The moray eel is an enemy of the octopus. It, too, likes to make a home in caves and crevices, especially

This spotted moray eel hides in a crevice in its ocean home. (Stephen Frink/WaterHouse)

in coral reefs. Its small pointed head peeks out from its shadowy hiding place. The moray's long, snakelike body curls and twines into the crevices, ready to dart out in an angry attack on any passing fish. A mouthful of sharp, strong teeth makes it a danger to any passerby.

Some morays grow as long as six feet (nearly two meters), but the common spotted moray only reaches a length of three feet (about one meter). Even small morays are so powerful that most anglers would rather cut their lines than land one in a boat. The sharp teeth make a wicked bite, and the heavy, thrashing body can bruise an unwary hand or foot.

Not satisfied with living peacefully in its own cave or crevice, the moray invades others looking for food. An octopus whose home a moray enters soon becomes the moray's dinner.

Toadfish

A thrown-away can or jar on the bottom of a shallow bay often becomes the home of a toadfish. There is nothing pretty about this thick, mud-colored creature. Its huge mouth is set in a broad, flat head. Black eyes look out from bulging sockets. Short, fleshy projections hang from the lower lip and parts of the head. Strong jaws and blunt teeth give the toadfish the tools it needs to snap up any passing food. Fortunately for the toadfish, it has an appetite that matches its many meals.

The toadfish lurks lazily in its home, watching for small sea creatures to wander by. With a snap and a gulp it swallows the creature, and then settles back to wait for another. The toadfish attacks its food with such power that it will completely swallow the bait and hook of any angler unlucky enough to catch one.

Such a lazy, hungry creature is bound to get fat. Some toadfish have been known to live in glass jars on the sea bottom. This home works well until the animal suddenly discovers that it has eaten too much to be able to get out the narrow opening of the jar. Then the toadfish is homebound for life, hoping enough curious sea creatures pass by to keep it well fed.

The creatures that live in caves, crevices and cans do not like to be disturbed. To avoid trouble, it is wise not to poke around in these homes in the sea. You can guess what may happen if you do.

② Rocks and Docks

Rocks and the pilings of docks are homes for creatures that can stick and stay. Waves pound and crash against these sea homes. Tides rise and fall, at times leaving the areas exposed to the air and the heat of the sun. Yet some creatures are especially adapted to living in such conditions. Barnacles, mussels, and limpets each have different means of attaching tightly to a rock or dock home. Each has a hard shell to protect its soft body from waves, wind, and sun.

Barnacles

Acorn or rock barnacles can be found along almost any shore. Masses of these creatures form white, crusty blankets across the face of rocks and around dock pilings. Any hard, smooth surface can become a home for barnacles. They will attach to the bottoms of boats, the shells of sea turtles, and even the tough, thick skin of a whale.

The barnacle begins life as a free-swimming **larva**

Barnacles have attached to the thick skin of this gray whale. (Stan Minasian/EarthViews)

These rock barnacles form a crusty blanket on the shores of the Maine coast in Acadia National Park. (James P. Rowan)

that looks nothing like the adult. In about three months, after several changes in shape, the tiny creature finds a suitable place to settle down. Its chosen home is usually near, or even on, other barnacles.

Landing on its head, the baby barnacle **secretes**, or gives off, a strong cement that attaches it firmly in place. Then it builds a cone of shell plates around its body. The top of the cone is open, like the crater of a volcano. Inside the opening, more shell plates form a valve, or door, that closes to protect the barnacle from drying out when the tide is low. To eat, the barnacle opens its valves and thrusts out six pairs of feathery legs. These form a net which scoops up **microscopic** particles of food from the water.

The rock or acorn barnacle may grow as large as two inches (about five centimeters), but most are no larger than a dime or nickel. Whatever their size, the top edges of barnacle shells are sharp. For that reason, swimmers should stay away from dock pilings or barnacle-covered rocks along the shore.

Blue Mussel

Blue mussels often share space with barnacles. They, too, cluster together in large masses, forming a blue-black blanket of shells. Mussels are **bivalves**, or animals with two shells. The shells close tightly to protect the soft animal inside. They open to allow seawater to pass over the mussel's **gills**, which filter out microscopic plants for food and oxygen for breathing.

Strong, silken threads attach mussels to their homes. Each mussel secretes a sticky fluid that hardens in the water, forming the threads that spread out from the shell's pointed end like the ropes of a tent. If a thread breaks, the mussel can make another. It can even shift its position very, very slowly. First it attaches several anchor threads in the direction it wants to move. Then, one step at a time, it pulls itself along like a mountain climber pulling up on a rope. All the mussel needs for a home is a tiny space to anchor its threads, and room enough to open its shell slightly to the seawater.

Masses of mussels and barnacles form sharp little shell cities on rocks and dock pilings. Other tiny sea creatures swim or crawl among the shells as they look for shelter and food. Currents of seawater wash over the mussels and barnacles, bringing the microscopic particles these creatures need for their own food.

Masses of blue mussel shells cover this spot on the Maine coast. (Lynn Stone)

Limpets

Limpets also live on rocks and smooth surfaces. But unlike mussels and barnacles, they prefer to live alone. Limpets look like tiny brownish or gray cone-shaped shell mountains clinging to the face of rocks. A strong, flat muscular foot acts like a suction cup to attach the limpet to its home. Each limpet has its own special spot that has been ground down to make a perfect airtight seal with the shell. So tightly do these little one- to two-inch-long creatures cling that a person cannot pull them loose. It takes a sharp knife slipped quickly under the shell to break loose the strong seal of a limpet.

Unlike barnacles and mussels, limpets do not wait for the sea to bring them food. Instead, they move out from their homes to graze, like a horse in a pasture. When the tide is high, the limpet pulls itself along the rock surface on its large foot. Its tongue, or **radula**, is fitted with tiny teeth that scrape up tiny plants called algae. The limpet leaves a clear path wherever it goes, scraping the area so thoroughly that bits of rock may end up in its stomach.

After eating, the limpet returns to its home spot. No matter what direction a limpet moves, it always

These limpets have scraped out smooth spots in a large rock to make their home. Unlike most limpets, they live together in a small group.

seems to know where to find the small groove or scar that marks its home.

The clinging creatures of rocks and docks flourish despite the threat of being washed away or crushed by crashing waves. They are well adapted to their special homes.

The Surface of the Sea

Imagine spending your life dangling from a balloon or hanging upside down. The surface of the sea is home for some creatures that live floating beneath their own rafts or balloons.

Purple Sea Snail (Janthina)

The purple sea snail, or Janthina, is a raft builder. It secretes a sticky fluid that traps bubbles of air. The clear fluid hardens, forming a bubble raft that floats on the top of the sea. The snail, which is no bigger than your thumb, hangs upside down from the bottom of the raft. It eats, breathes, and lives out its life in this position. When the female lays eggs, she attaches them to the bottom of the raft beside her.

When large groups of Janthinas float together, their bubble rafts look like foam on top of the sea. These sea snails eat microscopic animals that float in the sea and other small creatures that may venture near the surface. If disturbed, Janthinas release a purple fluid. If storm waves toss them ashore, their purple dye may streak the sand where they and their rafts have landed.

Portuguese Man-of-War

The Portuguese man-of-war has its own gas-filled balloon that floats on the surface of the sea. The sky-blue balloon is topped with a ridge or crest that acts like a sail in the wind. Dangling beneath the balloon are streamers of various colors. The most dangerous are the long, purple-tinted stinging tentacles. They may hang down into the sea as deep as a ten-story building is tall. Yet the balloon that supports them is only between three and twelve inches (about eight to thirty-two centimeters) long.

Each stinging tentacle contains thousands of cells that release a powerful poison when touched. The man-of-war spreads its tentacles like a net to catch fish for food. Swimmers and divers may be badly hurt if they bump into the tentacles.

The Portuguese man-of-war is found in warm tropical seas and often washes ashore. Its bright balloons may dot the beach, but even dead, its poison cells can still work. Its major enemy is the Janthina snail. If the

raft of a Janthina and the balloon of a man-of-war come together, you can be sure the Janthina is having a good meal.

For animals that float on the surface of the sea, home is wherever the winds and the waves move them. Sometimes they float peacefully on a calm sea. Sometimes they are bounced about by rough waves. In a storm, they may be tossed ashore and lose their homes altogether.

Viewed from underwater, a Portuguese man-of-war floats on the surface of the sea. Its long, stinging tentacles hang down into the ocean. (Stephen Frink/WaterHouse)

 The Open Sea

Fish, jellyfish, and sea mammals roam the open sea, like cattle on the range. From shore to shore, and as deep as the light of the sun can penetrate, the sea offers a vast pasture. Billions of tiny plants and animals, too small for the eye to see, float in the ocean. These are the **plankton**, the basic food of the sea.

The tiny plants are eaten by tiny animals and by some of the larger animals, also. Tiny animals are eaten by larger meat-eating animals. These, in turn, are eaten by even larger animals.

Like the ever-moving waters of the sea, creatures of the open sea constantly move in their search for food, safety, and the right temperature and light. The most familiar to us are the fish.

Fish

Of all the animals in the sea, fish are the most numerous. Saltwater fish are much like those in fresh water, except they need the salt to live.

These spadefish travel together in a school in the Fiji Islands of the South Pacific Ocean. (Jacki Kilbride/EarthViews)

Fish are **vertebrates,** or animals with backbones. They breathe through gills, which take oxygen from the water much as our lungs take oxygen from the air. Their fins serve as paddles and sails and keels to help them move and balance in the water. With their streamlined bodies, fish can speed through the sea or wait almost motionless in a single spot.

Fish often travel in large groups called **schools** or

shoals. They may migrate from one area to another to follow warm or cool temperatures or the food supply. There are many different kinds of fish. They vary greatly in size, shape and color. One may be no longer than your thumbnail, while another may be as long as a city bus. The names of some fish tell you something about their shapes. Would you recognize a swordfish or a hammerhead shark if you saw one?

Sharks

Of all the fish that roam the open sea, the sharks are the most fearsome. One look at the huge mouth and sharp, pointed teeth of a great white shark is enough to scare anyone. This thirty-foot (nine-meter) giant is feared because it has attacked people. However, it, like most other sharks, feeds mainly on fish. Since sharks probably cannot tell the difference between a person and a large fish, it is best not to be around when a shark is hungry!

In fact, shark attacks on people are rare, especially during daylight hours at public beaches. A person is in much greater danger of being injured in an automobile accident on the way to the beach than by a shark attack at the beach.

Using its flippers on each side, a huge, diamond-shaped manta ray speeds through the sea. (Jacki Kilbride/EarthViews)

Manta Ray

The manta ray is a huge, diamond-shaped fish of the open sea. Its wide, flat body can be broader than a small boat. Flippers on each side move like huge wings, propelling the ray through the water. Two hornlike projections on its head and a whiplike tail add to its strange appearance.

Though it has a threatening look, the manta ray is

a harmless creature that feeds on small ocean life. Playful at times, it has been known to leap out of the water and splash down in a loud belly flop. Such a sight has frightened people fishing in a small boat.

Dolphins and Whales

Dolphins and whales look like fish, but they aren't fish at all! They are **mammals**, or warm-blooded animals, like the fur-bearing animals on land. Other sea creatures are cold-blooded, having blood the same temperature as the surrounding water. Since whales and dolphins have no fur to keep them warm, their bodies have a thick layer of fat, or blubber.

They cannot breathe oxygen from the water, since they have **lungs** like land animals, instead of gills like fish. Dolphins and whales must rise to the surface to breathe. If they don't, they will drown. Old air is blown out through a blowhole in the top of the head, and fresh air is taken in. When a whale breathes out, the warm, moist air from its lungs forms a column of vapor that looks like a spout of water.

The blue whale is the largest animal in the world. It can grow 110 feet (33.5 meters) long—as long as two buses! Although it weighs as much as 150 tons (135

A pack of graceful killer whales moves together along the surface of the sea near land. (Ken Balcomb/EarthViews)

metric tons), the blue whale floats on the sea as easily as a rubber raft. In spite of its size, this gentle creature feeds on plankton and small sea creatures.

Although the much smaller killer whale grows no longer than thirty feet (nine meters), it is the most dangerous of all whales. Hunting in packs, it attacks large sea animals, including the huge, but defenseless, blue whale. The killer whale is a beautiful animal, with smooth and shiny jet black skin on its back and sides and bright white underparts.

Several killer whales have been captured while young and raised in **seaquariums**. They have been trained to perform a number of tricks on command, and will even allow a person to ride on their backs as they swish through the water.

The beauty and grace of these killers of the sea make them popular attractions at seaquariums that provide shows for the public. When raised and trained in captivity, killer whales usually do not threaten humans if kept well fed. No matter how tame it appears, however, the killer whale is still a wild animal.

The killer whale is really more closely related to dolphins than whales. Dolphins, too, have become popular performers in sea shows. More intelligent and active than whales, dolphins are not hard to tame and easily learn many tricks. They are affectionate toward people and enjoy the attention of their trainers.

Dolphins have a highly developed language. In the sea they use a number of different sounds to communicate with each other. When a dolphin is in trouble, its distress call brings others rapidly to its aid.

In their natural ocean home, dolphins are friendly,

Two bottlenose dolphins leap above the ocean waves. (Robert Pitman/ EarthViews)

playful creatures. They travel in groups, often following ships and playing about in the water. They can
leap completely out of the sea in a graceful arc. They
can even rise straight up out of the water, head high,
and give the appearance of walking on their tails for
short distances.

Jellyfish

While the open sea is home for the most intelligent
of the ocean creatures, it is also home for a group of
animals that has no brains at all. The jellyfish spends
its life moving slowly through the water. In spite of its
name, it is not really a fish, since it has no bones. Its
body is a jellylike mass—called a **medusa**—that looks
somewhat like an umbrella. Most have long, stinging
tentacles which trap small fish for food.

Some jellyfish are colorless, almost invisible in
the sea. Others are delicate shades of pink, blue, red,
or purple. Flower or cross-shaped designs stand out on
some of the umbrellas.

Jellyfish move by partially closing and opening
the umbrella, drawing in and pushing out water in a
regular, constant motion. So weak is the movement,
however, that jellyfish are easily tossed about by the

*This jellyfish lives in the Marine Lakes of the islands of Palau in the
South Pacific Ocean. (Jacki Kilbride/EarthViews)*

waves and tides. Their slow, pulsing movement does keep them from sinking into the darkness of the deep sea, where they would soon die.

The great red jellyfish is the largest of these creatures. It lives far out in the sea, where there is plenty of room for its 7-foot-wide (2.2-meter-wide) body and 100-foot-long (30.5-meter-long) tentacles to move freely. Jellyfish near shore are much smaller. Whatever their size, their long tentacles can give a painful sting.

The slow moving jellyfish, the streamlined, swiftly swimming fish, and the intelligent mammals are all at home in the huge range of the open sea.

 # The Deep Sea

The deep sea is cold, dark, and still—a forbidding place to live. Because no sunlight can penetrate its depths, no plant life can grow. The microscopic sea pasture of the open sea is no longer available for food. At less than a half mile (eight-tenths kilometer) down, the pressure of the water is great enough to crush a person's ribs. Yet in this sunless, desolate world, many sea creatures thrive. Their bodies are adapted for life in the deep. They feed on particles that drift down from above—or on each other.

Lantern Fish

In the darkness of the deep, many creatures create their own lights. The lantern fish has special organs made of light-producing cells that line the sides of its body. As they shine, bright dots of white, blue, yellow, green, or red glow in the dark. The little three-inch (eight-centimeter) fish may have a hundred lanterns glowing, giving it the look of a tiny ocean liner sailing through the sea. Each different **species**, or kind, of lantern fish has its own special pattern of lights. The patterns help it to recognize its own kind in the darkness of its home.

Angler Fish

The angler fish is a fish that goes fishing. It has what looks like a fishing rod growing from the top of its head. A little bit of skin or muscle dangles from the end like bait, hanging down in front of the angler's mouth. One kind of angler even has a bait that is lighted. The broad, flattish angler flutters its bait until another fish comes to investigate. As soon as the unsuspecting victim gets close enough, the angler quickly sucks it in.

Only the female angler can fish. The little male bites into the two- or three-foot-long female and latches on for life. Since the male angler's body actually becomes a part of the female's, the male receives all its food through the female.

Life in the Deep Sea

There is still much to be learned about life in the deep sea. We know that many of these creatures create

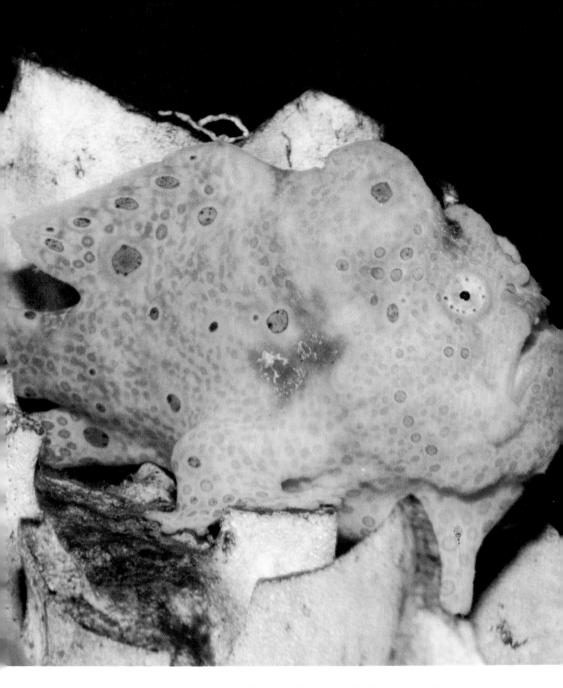

The strange-looking angler fish dangles a bit of skin or muscle from its own head as bait to attract other fish. (James P. Rowan)

their own lights and that some have special methods for attracting food. We also know that many deep sea creatures have huge, bulging eyes, possibly helping them to find the lighted creatures. Others are blind and depend upon long, sensitive feelers to find their way around.

At deeper levels in the sea, food becomes scarcer. The ability of some fish to swallow huge amounts of food at one time makes up for the long periods they must go without a meal. Their mouths are large, opening wider than the fish itself. Some even have stomachs that stretch to hold other fish several times larger than themselves.

There are creatures of the deep sea yet to be discovered. About many others we know very little. Specially designed submarines take scientists into the deepest parts of the ocean to explore. They have found life of some kind at more than 6.5 miles (10.5 kilometers) in depth. The dark of the deep sea may seem forbidding, but to some creatures it is home.

6 Sand and Mud

The sea bed is home for more different kinds of creatures than any other part of the sea. If you look at the sand or mud in shallow waters near shore, you may think it is lifeless. The creatures here are hidden, buried beneath the sand or mud. If you look closely in still waters, you may see tiny tracks or paths across the bottom. These are the trails of little animals—perhaps a snail, a starfish, or a sand dollar. You may also see tiny holes in the sand leading to the homes of other creatures—possibly a clam or a marine worm.

Even in the heavy surf of ocean shores, you may see, or more likely feel, evidence of life. As you walk, a fish or a crab may scurry away from beneath your feet.

Clams

Clams are creatures of the sand and mud. These bivalves, or animals with two shells, are specially equipped to burrow or dig. The clam has a strong, muscular, hatchet-shaped foot. It pushes the pointed end

The two shells of this file clam open to show its brightly colored layers inside. (James P. Rowan)

of the foot as deep into the sand as it will go. Then a strange thing happens. The clam pumps blood into the foot until the end swells into a mushroom-shaped bulb. The bulb serves as an anchor while the clam pulls itself down and over the foot. Then down goes the foot again, and out comes the anchor, over and over until the clam is well buried.

The clam must have a way to breathe from under

the sand. Again, it is well equipped. Two tiny tubes, or **siphons**, are pushed up to the water. One tube inhales, or draws in, seawater and passes it across the clam's gills. The gills filter out oxygen and microscopic plants. The water, and any waste, is exhaled, or pushed out, the second siphon. Buried in the sand or mud, the clam is well adapted to live in its particular marine environment.

Oysters

Oysters are bivalves that live in beds—but these are not the soft beds we know. Hundreds of grayish, sharp-edged shells are attached over, under, and around each other, forming broad shell masses. Such a bed of oysters may stretch over large areas of shallow bays.

A gray blob of an animal lives inside each thick pair of shells. The oyster is a pump in miniature. It draws in gallons of seawater each day and filters out the tiny plants it needs for food. A strong muscle in the middle of its body attaches to both shells, opening and closing them.

The inside of the oyster's shell is smooth, shiny, and white, except for the small scar where the muscle is attached. The inside lining of the shell is called mother-of-pearl. If a grain of sand gets caught in the shell, it disturbs the oyster, just as something in your eye makes you want to rub it. To protect itself, the oyster covers the grain with layers of mother-of-pearl, thus forming a pearl.

Pearls of the common food oyster are interesting but not valuable. Pearl oysters are a separate species of bivalve. Divers go down into the sea to gather them for their valuable pearls.

Oysters are good to eat—so good, in fact, that some fishermen have developed oyster farms in the water. They spread clean, empty oyster shells on the sea bottom to form a bed for the baby oysters to settle on. Then they try to keep the water clean and protect the oysters from other creatures that would like to make a meal of them.

Marine Snails

Marine snails creep across the sea bed, leaving little trails wherever they go. These slow-moving creatures have a single shell twisted into a spiral. Some spirals are long and thin, while others are short and fat. Some also have knobs or spikes or other unusual shell shapes. One end of the shell is open. The snail's large foot and its head stick out as it wanders in search of food. When danger threatens, the snail closes itself in the shell, blocking the opening with a trap door called an **operculum**. It is attached to the foot.

Some snails are meat eaters that feed on oysters and clams. The moon snail's large foot helps it burrow into the sand and hold tightly to any clam it finds. It drills a hole through the clam's shell with its filelike tongue, or radula. In goes the long snout, or **proboscis**, sucking out the soft, juicy clam meat. The round, flattish moon snail looks like a small, sandy mound moving along under the surface of the sand.

Snails have no legs, but you may find a snail shell with a set of legs moving it around. If so, you have found a hermit crab. Since this creature cannot grow its own shell, it must look for the castoffs of snails. The hermit crab moves right into the empty snail shell. As soon as it grows a little, however, it must look for another, larger shell.

Often it is possible to find the shells of different kinds of snails and clams washed up on the seashore. Walking along the beach, you can observe many different shell sizes, shapes, and colors.

A hermit crab moves into the empty shell of a marine snail and makes it home until the crab grows too big for the shell. (James P. Rowan)

Crabs

Crabs scurry across the sea bottom, looking some-what like huge spiders with claws. The blue crab has blue claws and pale blue blood. Four pairs of legs carry it across the bottom or scoop a shallow nest in the sand. The back set of legs has what looks like little paddles on the end to help propel, or move, the crab when it wishes to swim.

Crabs have a hard covering or shell that is nothing like the shell of a snail or clam. It is more like a thin plate of armor covering the soft body parts. As the crab grows, it must shed its shell and grow another, larger one. Right after it has shed, the new shell underneath is soft. Many people find this softshell crab delicious to eat.

Until the new shell hardens, the crab has little means to protect itself other than its huge claws. If the claws are broken off, new claws will grow. This re-growth, or **regeneration**, of body parts is a characteristic of several sea creatures.

Starfish

The starfish can regenerate its arms. In fact, if a large enough piece of arm is separated from the body, it will grow into a whole new starfish. These five-armed creatures have an eye spot, sensitive to light, at the tip of each arm. The undersides of the arms are equipped with numerous tiny feet. In some kinds of starfish, the feet are suckers that can stick fast to any solid object. The sand-dwelling starfish has hundreds of pointed tube feet for digging into the sand. It can sink rapidly out of sight.

As harmless as it looks, the starfish is one of the greatest enemies of shellfish. Its favorite foods are oysters and clams. The starfish wraps around a bivalve and slowly pulls open the shell. Then it does something no other creature can do. It pushes its stomach into the shell, digests the victim, and pulls its stomach back into its own body. When it's hungry, then, the starfish sends its stomach out for food!

Sand Dollar

Sand dollars are relatives of the starfish. But these flat, thin, round little creatures have no arms or legs. For that matter, they have no eyes or brain, either. To look at one, you would wonder how it can move at all. Its shell-like skeleton is covered with tiny, soft, hairlike spines that look and feel almost like

A starfish has an eye spot at the tip of each of its five arms and numerous tiny feet on the arms' undersides. (Robert Commer/EarthViews)

a purplish brown velvet. Like tiny waves, the spines ripple across the sand dollar's body, pulling it slowly through the sand. As it moves, one edge dips under the sand. Soon the entire creature is hidden.

Since the sand dollar's mouth is in the middle of its underside, it can sift the sand for small particles of

food. On top it has five petal-shaped marks. These contain tiny threads that bring in oxygen from the water.

Sand dollars grow about as large as the palm of a person's hand. Colonies of them live and move together, sinking beneath the sand to escape the starfish that want them for food. When washed ashore, their spine coverings rapidly disappear, leaving the hard, grayish skeletons that soon bleach snow white.

Flounder

Some fish also choose the sand and mud as home. The flounder is a broad, flat fish with a knack for changing color to match the sand it rests upon.

As a baby, the flounder looks like any other fish, but as it settles down on the bottom a strange change takes place. It lies on one side, getting flatter and flatter. The eye on its bottom side slowly moves across the top of its head until it is beside the other eye. The flounder lies quietly, half hidden in the sand, with only its eyes moving. Since each eye can move independently of the other, the flounder can watch two different objects at the same time. This way it can stay on the lookout for small crabs and other little creatures it likes for food.

This bleached white skeleton of a sand dollar is surrounded by the shells of coquina clams. (Lynn Stone)

A stingray glides over the ocean floor. Its dangerous whiplike tail with two sharp, saw-edged spines trails behind its body. (Ken Howard/Earth-Views)

Stingray

The stingray is another flat fish of the sea bed. It is related to the huge manta ray of the open sea. The stingray's wide, triangular-shaped body is broader than it is long. Most of its width comes from the broad, flat fins that flap like the wings of a bird to carry it through the water.

The dangerous part of the stingray is its long,

whiplike tail. It is equipped with one or two sharp, saw-edged spines that are used like daggers. A wader unlucky enough to step on a stingray may get a painful wound when the stingray flips its tail and drives the dagger into a foot. Fortunately, stingrays are just as afraid of people as people are of them. From their sandy beds, they try to flap away quickly if a person gets too close.

Sand and mud hide many creatures. Most are harmless. Many, especially some of the clams and snails, are beautiful. All are especially adapted to their homes in the sea.

 Seaweeds

Moving strands of seaweed offer shelter to many creatures. Like the animals on land that find homes in grasses, bushes, and trees, sea creatures abound wherever plant life grows. There are more plants in the sea, including the plant plankton, than all the plants on land.

Seaweed comes in various shades of greens, browns and reds. Some have broad, flat leaves and look like their name, sea lettuce. The leaflike strands of others may be feathery, long and thin, thick and fat, oval, or mosslike. Seaweed may be only an inch or two high, or may grow 100 feet (30.5 meters) long, like the giant kelps.

Sea Horse

The sea horse is probably the most interesting inhabitant of the weeds. A true fish, it has a backbone like other fish. With its tiny, horselike head upright, it curls its tail tightly around a seaweed strand. A bony

Despite its strange appearance, the sea horse is a true fish. Most of the time it stays safely hidden in its seaweed home. (Stephen Frink/WaterHouse)

armor full of ridges and knobs covers the body, which may grow seven inches (eighteen centimeters) long.

Most of the time the sea horse is content to float wherever the motion of the seaweed takes it. If it decides to move, it can swim slowly. As it moves forward in its upright position, its tiny fin waves rapidly through the water.

Hidden in the weeds, the sea horse looks like another strand of seaweed. From the safety of its perch, it can suck in tiny creatures for food and hide from the larger fish that would like to eat it for dinner. Since each of its eyes can rotate in a different direction at the same time, the sea horse can watch its surroundings closely.

Sargassum Fish

In the warm waters of the Atlantic Ocean, masses of sargasso weed float freely, tossed about by waves and ocean currents. One part of the ocean is even called the Sargasso Sea for the large amount of sargasso weed floating there. This seaweed is the home of the sargassum fish, whose swimming ability is so poor that it needs a safe place to hide.

The little fish grows no longer than six inches (fifteen centimeters). It is well adapted to its home among the weeds. Its orange-brown spotted coloring matches the color of the seaweed. Ragged fins and waving bits of fleshy knobs look like the leaves and branches of its home.

On each side, the sargassum fish has a fin shaped like a little arm with a flipper hand. It hooks the fin over a branch of sargasso weed and holds fast, floating wherever the weed goes. Sometimes a section of weed will break loose and float to northern shores, carrying the little sargassum fish with it.

Bay Scallop

Most bivalves are blind. They have no reason to see, since they stay fastened to one spot or burrow in the sand. But hidden on the floor of grassy sea areas is a bivalve that can see and really moves around.

The bay scallop, like the octopus, uses a form of jet propulsion. It swims by rapidly opening and closing its shells as if it were biting the water. Spurts of water jet out on both sides of the hinge, sending the scallop hurtling forward. It can also move backwards, hinge end first. This is its escape motion, which is used when a hungry starfish or other creature threat-

A bay scallop (lower left) *lies partly covered by a sea anemone* (center) *and flanked by a baby starfish* (lower right). *(Allan Roberts)*

ens. The movement of a scallop is so powerful that it can leap out of a small pail of seawater.

Tiny blue eyes line the open shells of the scallop. When all is quiet, the scallop lies in the shelter of the weeds, its shells open. It filters microscopic plants from the seawater for food, as do other bivalves. But its beady eyes are constantly alert to any sudden shadow. Danger is never far away in this watery world.

A large queen conch shell stands on a beach in early morning light. (Lynn Stone)

Queen Conch

The queen conch also finds shelter and food beneath the canopy of sea grasses. A huge snail, the queen conch can grow ten to twelve inches (twenty-five to thirty centimeters) long. Its rough, heavy shell has knobby spirals and a wide, flat lip. The underside of the lip is a brilliant pink, shiny mother-of-pearl. Like the oyster, the queen conch can create a pearl around a grain of sand or other substance that irritates its soft body. The queen conch's pearl is pink.

The animal within the shell moves along the bottom on its large snail foot, thrusting itself forward with a leap and tumblelike motion. Two long tubes with eyes on the ends stick out front, carefully scanning the area ahead. The queen conch is a meat eater that searches the sea bottom for dead bits of fish or other animals. Unfortunately for the queen conch, its meat makes a delicious conch chowder for people.

The jungles and forests of the sea, like the jungles and forests of the land, are essential to the life of the sea and to the many creatures that make them home.

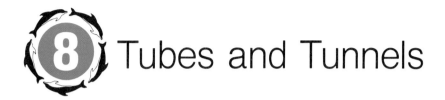

8 Tubes and Tunnels

Can you imagine seashells sinking a ship, a bivalve drilling a hole in a rock, or a worm building a tube in the sand? All these are sea creatures—the builders of tube and tunnel homes.

Shipworm

The shipworm does such a good job of tunneling into wood that groups of these tiny creatures have sunk many a ship. The adult shipworm can live only in wood, and wood does not grow in the sea. This sea creature's home must come to the sea from the land.

The free swimming baby shipworm has two tiny shells. It searches for a piece of wood—a log, the piling of a dock, or the bottom of a wooden ship. When it finds wood, the shipworm attaches an anchor thread similar to that of the mussel. Then its shells grow into sharp cutting blades with ridges on the edges. A strong muscle holds the shells together and scrapes them against the wood. The shipworm twists to the

right and then to the left, scraping against the wood with each movement. Day after day, scraping and twisting, it bores a tunnel at the rate of four inches (ten centimeters) a month. The tunnel may end up as long as eighteen inches (forty-eight centimeters).

The shipworm attaches the rear end of its body to the opening of the tunnel and holds fast. Two siphons reach out into the water for oxygen and food. The front end of the animal continues to scrape away with its tiny shells, while the body of the shipworm stretches out longer and thinner to reach between its two ends. No wonder it's called a worm. It certainly begins to look like one! But it is just another bivalve adapted to living in a very special situation.

As the shipworm bores, it lines its tunnel with a thin, hard layer of shell. The open end can be closed by two feathery extensions on the shipworm's rear end. When a threat appears, the tunnel becomes a safe, secure place. For a number of days, the shipworm can get the oxygen it needs from the water closed within the tunnel. For food, it can eat the wood scrapings until it is safe to open its door and draw in fresh water and the plankton it contains.

Huge numbers of shipworms may live in the same

This piece of wood from a ship has had many shipworm tunnels bored into it. (Allan Roberts) piece of wood. Yet they never invade each other's homes. As it bores into wood, the blind shipworm can somehow sense the presence of another tunnel. When it does, it simply moves off in a different direction to avoid it.

Piddocks

Piddocks are not so considerate of each other. These little bivalves bore into hard clay or even rock, scraping out tunnels much as the shipworms do. If one piddock runs into another piddock's home, though, that is soon the end of one of the creatures. One bores right on through the other and continues with its tunneling action.

The piddock uses its strong foot to hold tightly to the rock surface where it carves out its tunnel home. Strong muscles scrape the sawlike edges of the shell against the rock, digging deeper and deeper. The piddock does not stretch out its body like the shipworm. It stays within its shell, as most bivalves do, and moves completely into its tunnel. Hundreds of piddock holes may dot the side of a rock or cliff. Inside, these thumb-sized animals stay safely hidden within their homes.

Parchment Worm

The parchment worm chooses a softer place for its home. This marine worm tunnels into the sand of the sea bottom. It uses the slime from its body to build a U-shaped tube with two ends sticking out of the sand like tiny twin chimneys. Inside the tube lives the parchment worm, an animal that looks somewhat like a series of soft, flat seeds or flaps threaded together on a string. The flaps move like fans, pulling in a stream of plankton-filled seawater and pushing out the waste. As the worm grows, it lengthens the tube. If disturbed, it glows along its entire body with a bluish white light.

Tubes and tunnels serve as hideaway homes for the sea creatures that build them. Once in their safe homes, these creatures never leave unless they are forced to do so.

9 Animal Hosts

Some sea creatures find homes in or on other animals. They may settle in for life, gaining free room and board, or offering a cleaning service in return for their keep. Some are **parasites** that feed on their animal hosts.

Remora

One fish, the remora, is a hitchhiker. It can swim on its own, but prefers to attach itself to a shark or other large fish for a free ride. The top of the remora's head is covered with an oval, flat suction disk. Strong muscular flaps in the disk provide the suction needed to cling tightly to a swiftly swimming host fish. Mealtime for the host is mealtime for the remora, which grabs any leftover scraps that float its way.

Because of its ability to stick strongly, the remora was once used by American Indians to catch other fish and turtles. A cord was tied around the remora's tail, and it was thrown into the water. Since the re-

These two remoras have attached themselves to the head of a manta ray. (Marty Snyderman/WaterHouse)

mora does not like to be alone for long, it soon hitched onto a likely host. When the Indians pulled in the remora, in came the unwilling host, unable to detach itself from its unwelcome guest.

Remoras will grab a free ride on almost any large moving object, even boats and submarines. Perhaps they all look like fish to the remora. Imagine the surprise of scuba divers who suddenly find one- or two-foot-long fish attached to their legs, backs, or diving tanks. Remoras are harmless, however. When the divers leave the water, these hitchhiking fish will gladly search for other hosts to carry them through their underwater home.

Pea Crab

The drab little female pea crab finds lodging in the shells of mussels or scallops, or in the tubes of parchment worms. The round little body of the pea crab is about the size of a dime. Its shell and legs are soft, giving it little protection of its own.

Early in its life the pea crab finds a likely host. It spends its life snuggling safely in the host's shell or tube, where it gets the food it needs from the microscopic plants intended for the host. Since the pea crab does not cause any problems for its host, it is allowed to live its quiet life in relative peace.

Unlike the female, the male pea crab is an independent creature that floats freely in the sea. Its harder shell affords more protection than that of the female. When the male pea crab comes for a visit, it slips carefully into the female's lodging, and as quietly leaves again.

Sponges

While mussels and scallops offer lodging to single pea crabs, sponges become comfortable apartment houses for other creatures. Sponges are strange creatures themselves. They appear more like plants than animals but, as with many sea creatures, their appearance is deceiving. Sponges are usually colonies of many individuals so tightly bound together that they form a single large clump. The sponges you buy—if they are real sponges—are actually the skeletons of these animals.

Sponges hatch from eggs and swim about by means of **cilia**, tiny hairs which cover them. When an infant sponge is ready to settle down, it turns itself inside out. The cilia are then on the inside, where they can pull in the seawater for oxygen and food.

Sponge clumps grow into many different shapes, depending on the kind of sponge and its surroundings. The clumps stay attached to one place unless torn loose. Inside each one there are numerous openings and passages reaching into all parts of the sponge. To some small sea creatures, each opening is a tiny apartment—a perfect home with a constant flow of food-laden seawater.

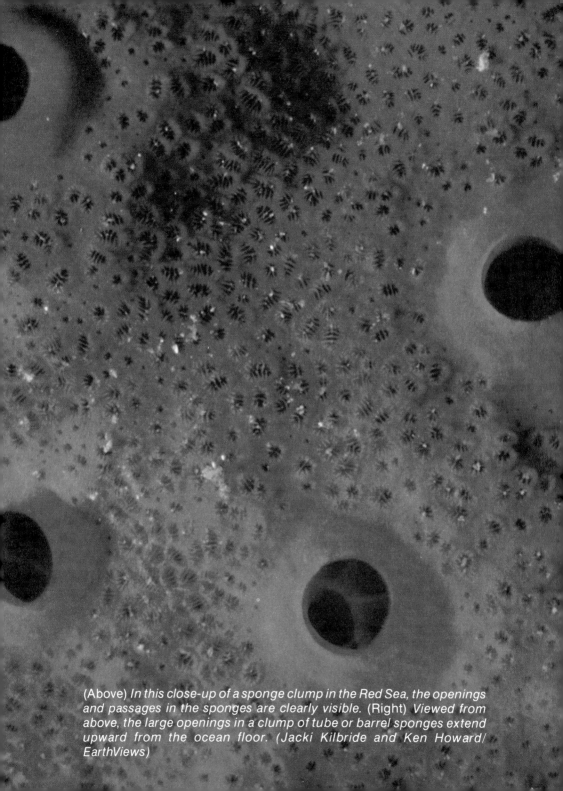

(Above) *In this close-up of a sponge clump in the Red Sea, the openings and passages in the sponges are clearly visible.* (Right) *Viewed from above, the large openings in a clump of tube or barrel sponges extend upward from the ocean floor. (Jacki Kilbride and Ken Howard/ EarthViews)*

Snapping Shrimp (Pistol Crab)

The snapping shrimp, or pistol crab, is often found living in sponges, especially the loggerhead sponge. This enormous, barrel-shaped sponge may grow as large as a tub and provide lodging for 15,000 snapping shrimp at a time. The unusual shrimp appears to be a cross between a shrimp and a crab, because it has a shrimplike body and a large crablike claw. The creature snaps its claw, making a sharp snapping noise. Such a loud, sudden sound must be frightening to other small creatures that invade the snapper's private passageway.

A loggerhead sponge full of snapping shrimp must be a noisy place to live. The shrimp do help their host, though, by keeping the sponge's passageways clean as they scrape food from its walls.

Parasitic Snails

Not all animal hosts are fortunate enough to have helpful, or at least harmless, house guests. **Parasitic** snails feed on their hosts. They especially like clams and mussels, and attach themselves to the bivalve near the open edge of its shells. The snail forces its long, needlelike sucker, or proboscis, through the shell opening and into the delicate meat of the clam. With a gentle pumping motion, it helps itself to the clam's blood.

Similarly, a mosquito may find that you offer a tasty meal if you fail to slap it in time. The clam, however, has no way of ridding itself of its unwelcome dinner guest. Perhaps, like a dog with fleas, it just learns to live with the pests.

Creatures using other animals for homes are affected by anything that affects the host. If the host moves, so does the lodger. If the host dies, the lodger must find a new home.

 Coral Reefs

If sponges are the apartment houses of the sea, and seaweeds the jungles, then coral reefs may be called the cities. They are cities built by tiny animals. The Great Barrier Reef of Australia is the largest structure ever built by living creatures. Yet the major builder may be as small as a pinhead, and is no larger than a fingernail.

Coral Polyps

Coral polyps are simple animals—nothing more than a tube closed at one end and surrounded by tiny tentacles at the other. These remarkable creatures are hidden inside hard, rocklike skeletons of lime. Billions of coral polyps cluster into colonies, forming group skeletons of many shapes.

The reef building corals build upon the skeletons of past generations. Over millions of years the skeletons, topped by living corals, become huge reefs. The largest, the Great Barrier Reef, is more than 1,250

This close-up of coral polyps shows that they have a tube closed at one end that leads to tiny, delicate tentacles at the other end. (Ken Howard/ EarthViews)

miles (2,000 kilometers) long—as long as the distance from New York City to Chicago. Smaller reefs cover many underwater areas in warm waters. Florida has its own living reef off the southern tip of the state.

Cities in the Sea

Coral reefs are much more than homes for the polyps that create them. They are centers of life for

Like hundreds of other sea creatures, these tropical fish find shelter in the caves and crevices formed by corals in a coral reef. (Allan Roberts)

hundreds of creatures that find shelter in the numerous caves and crevices formed by the corals. Snails, starfish, and creeping creatures cling to the hard lime rock and crawl around in search of food. Amazingly colorful tropical fish flit among the branches and tunnels formed by the coral. Larger fish seek the smaller fish as part of the endless food chain of the sea.

Plankton multiplies rapidly in the warm, sunlit

waters around coral reefs. It provides a constant source of food for small creatures and the ever hungry coral polyps. Masses of tiny tentacles cover the face of the reefs as the polyps feed. The constantly waving tentacles form brilliantly colored masses that look like undersea flower beds.

So abundant is the life around the reef cities that many creatures must share homes. Caves and crevices have their daytime dwellers and their nighttime dwellers. One set moves out to feed as the other moves in to rest. Like life in all parts of the sea, creatures adjust and adapt to the conditions available to them.

Homes in the sea are many and varied. The creatures that inhabit them are even more varied. Wherever they choose to live, though, their bodies and life habits fit them for their own special homes in the sea.

Appendix A:
Learning More About Sea Life

The following activities will help you learn more about sea life. Choose one or more to begin working on today.

1. Begin a notebook on sea life. Record your observations when you visit seashores or saltwater aquariums. Record any new or interesting facts you learn about the ocean and sea life. Write down any questions you have, and then look for answers in reference books, or ask a science teacher or other knowledgeable person. Record the answers. If you like to draw, add pictures of your favorite sea creatures.

2. Visit a seashore. A quiet bay is especially good. How many sea homes can you find? What kinds of creatures live in each? Look for holes or mounds on the sea bottom. Look on rocks, dock pilings, and plants that are washed by the salty water. Look carefully at seaweeds, driftwood, and even bottles or cans that have washed ashore. Do you see any evidence that some creature has lived in or on them? Are any creatures still there? Look for seashells. Where did they come from? Write your answers and observations in a notebook.

3. Visit a saltwater aquarium. If there is no large public seaquarium or oceanarium near you, check with museums, zoos, pet stores, and tropical fish stores. They will often have small saltwater aquariums. Observe the animals you see. Which are swimming around freely? Which stay on or near the bottom? Which hide in seaweeds, rocks, or shells? How far does each move from its chosen home? What differences in shape, color, and movement do you notice? Try to learn the names of each animal. Record your observations in a notebook.

4. Begin a collection of seashells. Small bottles can hold tiny shells. Boxes of various sizes, such as gift boxes and shoe boxes, are good for larger ones. Make dividers of cardboard to separate the different shells, or attach each shell to the box with a drop of glue. Look up the names of each kind of shell. Label each with its name and the date and place it was found. You can find your own shells, ask friends to send them to you, or purchase them. Find out more about the shells in your collection. What kind of home does each choose? You may wish to list interesting facts about each shell on its label.

Appendix B:
Scientific Names
for Sea Animals

Sea creatures, like all living things, have two kinds of names. The first is their *common name,* a name in the everyday language of an area where they are found. An animal often has a number of different common names in different languages. Also, several different animals may be known by the same common name.

The second kind of name is their *scientific name.* This is a Latin name assigned by scientists to identify an animal all over the world for other scientists. The scientific name is usually made up of two words. The first identifies a genus, or group, of similar animals (or plants), and the second identifies the species, or kind, of animal in the group. Sometimes, as scientists learn more about an animal, they may decide it belongs to a different group. The scientific name is then changed so that all scientists can recognize it and know exactly what animal it refers to.

If you want to learn more about the creatures in this book, the list of scientific names that follows will be useful to you. A typical species has been identified for each type of animal mentioned in the book. There may be many other species in the same group.

Chapter	Common Name	Scientific Name
1.	Common Octopus	*Octopus vulgaris*
	Spotted Moray Eel	*Gymnothorax moringa*
	Toadfish	*Opsanus beta*
2.	Acorn or Rock Barnacle	*Balanus balanoides*
	Blue Mussel	*Mytilus edulis*
	Cayenne Keyhole Limpet	*Diodora cayenensis*
3.	Purple Sea Snail	*Janthina janthina*
	Portuguese Man-of-war	*Physalia physalis*
4.	Great White Shark	*Carcharadon carcharias*
	Manta Ray	*Manta birostris*
	Blue Whale	*Balaenoptera musculus*
	Killer Whale	*Orcinus orca*
	Bottlenose Dolphin	*Tursiops truncatus*
	Sea Nettle Jellyfish	*Chrysaora quinquecirrha*
	Red Jelly	*Cyanea capillata*

Chapter	Common Name	Scientific Name
5.	Deep Sea Lantern Fish	*Myctophum affine*
	Deep Sea Angler Fish	*Cryptopsaras couesi*
6.	Quahog Clam	*Mercenaria mercenaria*
	Soft-shelled or Steamer Clam	*Mya arenaria*
	Eastern Oyster	*Crassostrea virginica*
	Atlantic Pearl Oyster	*Pinctada radiata*
	Moon Snail	*Lunatia heros*
	Long-clawed Hermit Crab	*Pagurus longicarpus*
	Blue Crab	*Callinectes sapidus*
	Common Sea Star	*Asterias forbesi*
	Northern Sea Star	*Asterias vulgaris*
	Keyhole Urchin Sand Dollar	*Mellita quinquiesperforata*
	Common Sand Dollar	*Echinarachnius parma*
	Southern Flounder	*Paralichthys lethostigma*
	Round Stingray	*Urolophus halleri*

Chapter	Common Name	Scientific Name
7.	Atlantic Sea Horse	*Hippocampus hudsonius*
	Sargassum fish	*Histrio histrio*
	Bay Scallop	*Argopecten irradians*
	Queen Conch	*Strombus gigas*
8.	Common Shipworm	*Teredo navalis*
	Flat-tipped Piddock	*Penitella penita*
	Great Piddock	*Zirfaea crispata*
	Parchment Worm	*Chaetopterus variopedatus*
9.	Remora	*Echeneis naucrates*
	Pea Crab	*Pinnotheres maculatus*
	Loggerhead Sponge	*Spheciospongia vesparia*
	Snapping Shrimp or Pistol Crab	*Synalpheus brooksi*
	Parasitic Snail	*Pyramidella fusca*

Chapter	Common Name	Scientific Name
10.	Reef Starlet Coral	*Siderastrea siderea*
	Porous Coral	*Porites astreoides*
	Pillar Coral	*Dendrogyra cylindrus*

 Glossary

bivalve (BUY-valv)—a shellfish that has two shells

cilia (SIL-ee-uh)—used here to mean tiny hairs covering infant sponges that move them through the water

corals—sea animals with hard, rocklike skeletons on the outside of their bodies; huge numbers of coral polyps massed together form coral reefs by building on the hardened skeletons of past generations

crevices (KREV-ih-sez)—narrow openings resulting from splits or cracks

environment—all the conditions surrounding and affecting an area; in the sea, temperature, light, wave action, salinity, depth, and amount of oxygen in the water are all important parts of the environment

gills—breathing organs that filter oxygen from seawater

larva—the early form of an animal that at birth or hatching is unlike its parent and must change before it becomes an adult

lungs—breathing organs in air-breathing animals

mammals—warm-blooded animals that nurse their young with milk from their own bodies

marine worms—worms that live in the sea

medusa (mih-DYU-suh)—a scientific name for the umbrellalike body form of a jellyfish

microscope—an instrument that magnifies objects too small to be seen clearly with the naked eye

microscopic (my-kro-SCOP-ik)—extremely small in size; an object that can be seen only with a microscope

operculum (oh-PURR-kyu-luhm)—the "trap door" used by a snail to block its shell opening when threatened

oxygen—a colorless, odorless, tasteless gas that all animals must breathe in order to live; it is in the air and is dissolved in seawater

parasites (PAHR-uh-sites)—often harmful creatures that live in or on other creatures

parasitic (pahr-uh-SIT-ik)—living on and feeding on another creature

plankton—tiny plants and animals that float in the sea; many are microscopic

proboscis (pruh-BAHS-uhs)—the long, tubelike snout of snails

radula (RAJ-uh-lah)—the ribbonlike tongue of a snail; it is covered with numerous tiny, sharp teeth

regeneration—regrowth of a part of the body that has been broken off

salinity (suh-LIN-it-ee)—used here to mean the salt content of seawater

school—used here to mean a large number of fish swimming together

seaquarium (see-KWAIR-ee-uhm)—a sea aquarium, or huge tank filled with seawater in which sea animals and plants can be viewed and studied

secrete (sih-KREET)—to form and give off a substance

shellfish—sea animals that have shells, such as clams and snails

siphon (SY-fuhn)—a tube in some sea animals used for drawing seawater into and out of the body

species (SPEE-sheez)—distinct kinds of individual plants or animals that have common characteristics and share a common name

sponges—plantlike sea animals bound together in masses; their dried skeletons are soft and absorb water, making them ideal for use in washing cars and other objects

tentacles (TEHN-tuh-kuhls)—armlike extensions on the body of a sea animal; used for moving, feeling, or grasping

vertebrates (VUHR-tuh-brayts)—animals with backbones

Selected Bibliography

Books

Burton, Maurice, ed. *The New Larousse Encyclopedia of Animal Life.* Revised ed. New York: Bonanza Books, 1984.

Carson, Rachel. *Edge of the Sea.* New York: Houghton Mifflin, 1955.

——. *The Sea Around Us.* New York: Oxford University Press, 1951.

Feinberg, Harold S., ed. *Simon & Schuster's Guide to Shells.* A Fireside Book. New York: Simon & Schuster, 1980.

Hylander, Clarence J. *Fishes and Their Ways.* New York: MacMillan, 1964.

Laurie, Alec. *The Living Oceans.* Garden City, New York: Doubleday, 1973.

Meinkoth, Norman A. *The Audubon Society Field Guide to North American Seashore Creatures.* New York, Alfred A. Knopf, 1981.

Sandved, Kjell B., and Abbott, R. Tucker. *Shells in Color.* New York: Viking, 1973.

Soule, Gardner. *Remarkable Creatures of the Sea.* New York, G.P. Putnam's, 1975.

Articles

Earle, Sylvia A. "Undersea World of a Kelp Forest." *National Geographic*, September 1980, pp. 411-426.

Linehan, Edward J. "The Trouble with Dolphins." *National Geographic*, April 1979, pp. 506-540.

Whitehead, Hal. "The Unknown Giants." *National Geographic*, December 1984, pp. 774-789.

 Index

The photographs are reproduced through the courtesy of Earth-Views (Ken Balcomb, Robert Commer, Ken Howard, Jacki Kilbride, Stan Minasian, and Robert Pitman, photographers), Marine Mammal Fund; Allan Roberts; James P. Rowan; Lynn Stone; and WaterHouse (Stephen Frink and Marty Snyderman, photographers). Cover photo: Clownfish in anemone (Robert Commer/EarthViews).

About the Author

Jean Sibbald's interest in sea life started in childhood when, as the daughter of a marine biologist, she grew up on a marine biological station. Although her career has taken other directions since then, she was and is an avid amateur conchologist.

Homes in the Sea, says the author, "introduces young readers to the fascinating world of the sea in a manner designed to arouse their interest and curiosity. Never again will the sea be merely an expanse of water. For the reader, a visit to the seashore will become a search for sea homes."

Ms. Sibbald's educational background includes an undergraduate major in biology and a bachelor's and master's degree in speech communication. Currently she is a district staff development and training manager for the Florida Department of Health and Rehabilitative Services. The mother of two children, she lives in Tampa, Florida.